MARINA AROMSHTAM

The Real Boat

ILLUSTRATED BY
VICTORIA SEMYKINA

TRANSLATED FROM RUSSIAN BY OLGA VARSHAVER

templar publishing

A paper boat was sailing around in a pond.
The pond seemed very big and deep to the little boat.
When the breeze blew, ripples ran across the surface
and rocked him.

He felt very happy.

Two googly-eyed frogs were sitting on the bank.

"Croak! Croak-croak?" asked one.
"Croak-croakity-croak," answered the other.

In frog language this meant:

"Look! What's that? Where did that come from?"

"Humans are always throwing rubbish in the water."

But the paper boat could speak frog language.

"I'm not rubbish! I'm a boat!"

"A boat?" the frogs wondered. "Croak! What's a boat?

Why are you a boat?"

A duck landed in the water.

"What are you all doing here?" she asked.

"Croak! That thing there claims that he's a boat."

"Quack!" said the duck. She thought for a minute,
then said "quack" again.

"Once, a long time ago, I flew to the tropics."

"And why should we care?" replied the frogs.

"When I was flying," said the duck, "I saw real boats.
Sailing on the ocean."

"What's an ocean?" asked the paper boat.

"Quack! The ocean has lots and lots of water."

"Even more than we have here?" asked the frogs in amazement.

"Quack! The ocean has so much water that it joins the sky."

"Real boats sail on the ocean. I want to sail there too, just like a real boat!" thought the paper boat, and he called out, "So long! I'm going to the ocean."

Croak

A little stream trickled out of the pond and the paper boat
sailed along it, with the frogs behind him.

"Croak-croak! We're boats, too. We're going to the ocean."

But before long, the frogs got tired, and the paper boat sailed on alone.

The stream got wider and wider.

"Wow! There's so much water!" marvelled the paper boat.
"Now that must be the ocean!" But he didn't want to be wrong.
There was a rowboat near the riverbank and the paper boat
bobbed alongside.

"Could you be so kind as to tell me . . ." he began.
"Shhh! Don't be so noisy!" grumbled the old rowboat.
"You're quite lively, aren't you? You'll scare away
all the fish!"

"Could you be so kind as to tell me where the ocean is?"
said the paper boat, trying to whisper.
"Ocean? Never heard of it. Go away! I won't catch any fish
with you shouting like that."

"What a grump!" thought the paper boat,
and he went on his way.

After a while, the stream joined another stream and became a river.
The banks were even further away now. A motorboat roared past.

"Tell me, please, how can I get to the ocean?" called out the paper boat.
But the motorboat was already gone.

Soon, a riverboat came around the bend. The paper boat thought it was just lovely – how delightful it would be to sail along with music playing!

But the riverboat didn't know the way to the ocean.
"I just take passengers up and down the river from one stop
to the next. Ask someone over there."

Over there, in the distance, was a barge piled
high with sand.

When the barge got closer, the paper boat said to her, shyly,
"You must be really strong, to carry so much sand!"
"I can carry gravel, too," said the barge proudly,
"and sometimes even coal!"

The paper boat suddenly realised that the barge wasn't moving by itself –
a small, sturdy boat was pushing it from behind, huffing and puffing.

Chug Chug Chug Chug

"Now *you* really are a strong boat!" said the paper boat with admiration.

"I'm a tugboat. I chug along all right, but I can't go very fast,"
answered the tugboat. "What do you want, little one?"

"Do you know how to get to the ocean?"

"I'm taking this barge to the port. You can come if you like.
Someone there will know."

The paper boat pulled alongside the tugboat and tried to
huff and puff just like him.

~ Toot

The river grew wider and wider and fancy yachts
glided up and down with their bright sails.

Finally, the tops of tall cranes appeared in the distance,
and then – ships! Lots and lots of ships! Passenger liners,
container ships, fishing trawlers, cargo ships.
White seagulls flew overhead. It was a breathtaking sight!

"Soon we'll be getting into the harbour," explained the tugboat. "Then I'll take the barge to the dock to be unloaded. You go and find yourself someone who knows the way to the ocean. Goodbye, little one! **Chug-a-chug! Toot, toot!**"

There was so much to see in the harbour!

The ships were loaded and unloaded. Tall cranes raised and lowered shipping containers as big as whole rooms.

In one of these there were two spotted giraffes. A crane picked the container up as though it was full of nothing but cotton wool, and carefully set it down on the dock.

A big ferry boat was tied up at the wharf. One end swung open and formed a ramp. A car drove out, then another, and another, and another.

The paper boat counted the cars up to a hundred (which was as high as he could count) and still they kept coming.

There was so much to see that the paper boat
didn't notice it was getting dark.

Soon lights came on all over the port and a passenger
liner shone like an enchanted city.

"What an amazing ship! He's probably heading
for the ocean tomorrow. I'll go with him!" decided
the paper boat as he drifted off to sleep.

But when the paper boat woke up, the passenger liner
was already leaving the harbour.
"Toot, too-oo-oot, I'll be back soo-oo-oon,"
whistled the huge liner in parting, and soon he was gone.

"Cheer up, little one," a fishing trawler called out.
"Uhh . . . you wouldn't be going to the ocean,
would you?" asked the paper boat.
"Well of course I am!"
"I want to go to the ocean, too. Can I follow you?"
"Come along! But be careful not to get caught up
in my net like a fish!" the trawler laughed.
And the paper boat sailed behind him.

All of a sudden, the paper boat saw
something strange and frightening.
Smokestacks rose from the water
like parts of a sea monster's body.

"That thing you're afraid of is
a loading dock for tankers,"
the trawler said. "Look over there!
That is my old friend Supertanker.
See that big pump filling him full
of oil?"

Tied up next to the loading dock
was a ship as big as an island.

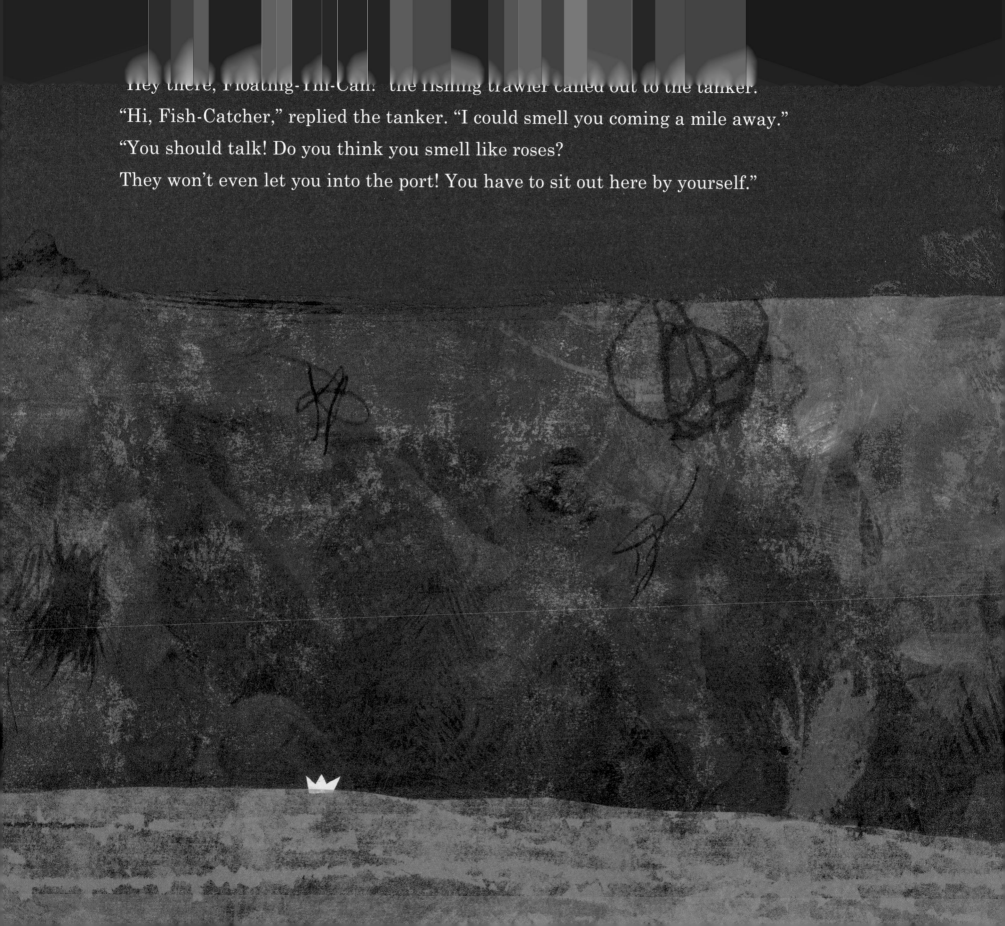

"Hey there, Floating-Fin-Can!" the fishing trawler called out to the tanker.

"Hi, Fish-Catcher," replied the tanker. "I could smell you coming a mile away."

"You should talk! Do you think you smell like roses?

They won't even let you into the port! You have to sit out here by yourself."

Well you take good care of your belly. You don't want even a drop of oil to spill into the sea. See you later, Floating-Tin-Can! The fish will be wondering where I am!"

"Goodbye for now, Fish-Catcher," said the tanker.

The port grew smaller and smaller in the distance. They couldn't even see ships any more, only the cranes. And soon even those disappeared and there was no land in sight – just water and more water, stretching to the sky.

The paper boat was sailing on the ocean, on the real ocean! He bounced on the waves, and splashed. He even tried to whistle like an ocean liner, but he could only make a funny little beep.

After a while, dark clouds appeared on the horizon. They moved across the sky like sharks, swallowing everything in their path. First they swallowed up the fluffy white clouds, then the sun, and finally the last little slice of blue sky.

Blinding bolts of lightning flashed and there were deafening roars of thunder.

The water turned black – as black as the sky – and the waves grew bigger.

The paper boat was tossed high and then came crashing down.

"Where are you, little one?" called the trawler. "Try to stay close to me!"

Just then, a huge wave caught the paper boat and carried him far away.
Then came another wave, even bigger and scarier.

Where could the waves be taking him?

When the storm had passed, the trawler was nowhere
to be seen. The sea grew calm and sunlight danced on the
still water. The paper boat was very frightened. The storm had
battered him badly and he was all alone on the huge ocean.

Just then, an unknown ship came out of the fog like a ghost.
It had antennas and radar transmitters and rockets
sticking out everywhere.

It was one of the naval fleet's destroyers. The destroyer seemed unhappy – cold and expressionless – and the paper boat didn't dare speak to him.

The destroyer disappeared back into the fog, as though he had never been there at all.

The paper boat was now completely filled with water,
and he had started to sink. As he sank deeper into the ocean,
there was less and less light and the water pressed down
on him more and more.

Finally he could go no further – he had reached the ocean floor.
He sighed sadly: "Will I spend the rest of time down here
among the fish?"

But he was wrong. Not far away, something strange was
blinding the creatures of the deep with a bright spotlight.

"Did you sink, too?" asked the paper boat
shyly. Are we partners in misfortune?"

"We're not partners of any sort! I am a submarine.
I come down here whenever I want. And then when
I want to, I go back up," replied the submarine,
and she rose towards the surface.

The paper boat was left alone again.
  "Before long, I'll be completely covered in sand,"
            he thought sadly.

But who was this in the water? A man in a diving suit!

"Here is a paper boat! Would you believe it?" thought the diver.

"Captain, here's a gift from the sea."
The diver, climbing back on board the research ship,
handed the paper boat to his captain.

That evening the captain took the paper boat to his cabin.
"How in the world did you wind up at the bottom of the ocean?
A shipwreck, perhaps?" The captain sighed.
"That can happen. It's just that you're so tiny –
and you've sailed so far!

A true seafarer!
A real boat!"

The captain cut a little plaque out of cardboard
and wrote on it in fancy letters:

INTREPID

Then he glued the plaque onto the side of the paper boat.

"You have earned this name by virtue of your journey,"
said the captain, and he put the little boat on the shelf
where everyone could see him.

"When we get home, I'll give you to my son.
He wants to be a sailor when he grows up."
The paper boat sighed happily.

He was a **real boat** with a **real name!**

For my grandsons Sam and Gorge
who I wish to become real boats – MA

A TEMPLAR BOOK

First published in the UK in 2017 by Templar Publishing,
an imprint of Kings Road Publishing, part of the Bonnier Publishing Group,
The Plaza, 535 King's Road, London, SW10 0SZ
www.bonnierpublishing.com

Text copyright © 2017 by Marina Aromshtam
Illustration copyright © 2017 by Victoria Semykina
Design copyright © 2017 by The Templar Company Limited

1 3 5 7 9 10 8 6 4 2

ISBN 978-1-78370-820-8

This book was typeset in Century Schoolbook

Designed by Maya Schleifer and Genevieve Webster
Edited by Katie Haworth and Beverly Michaels

Printed in China

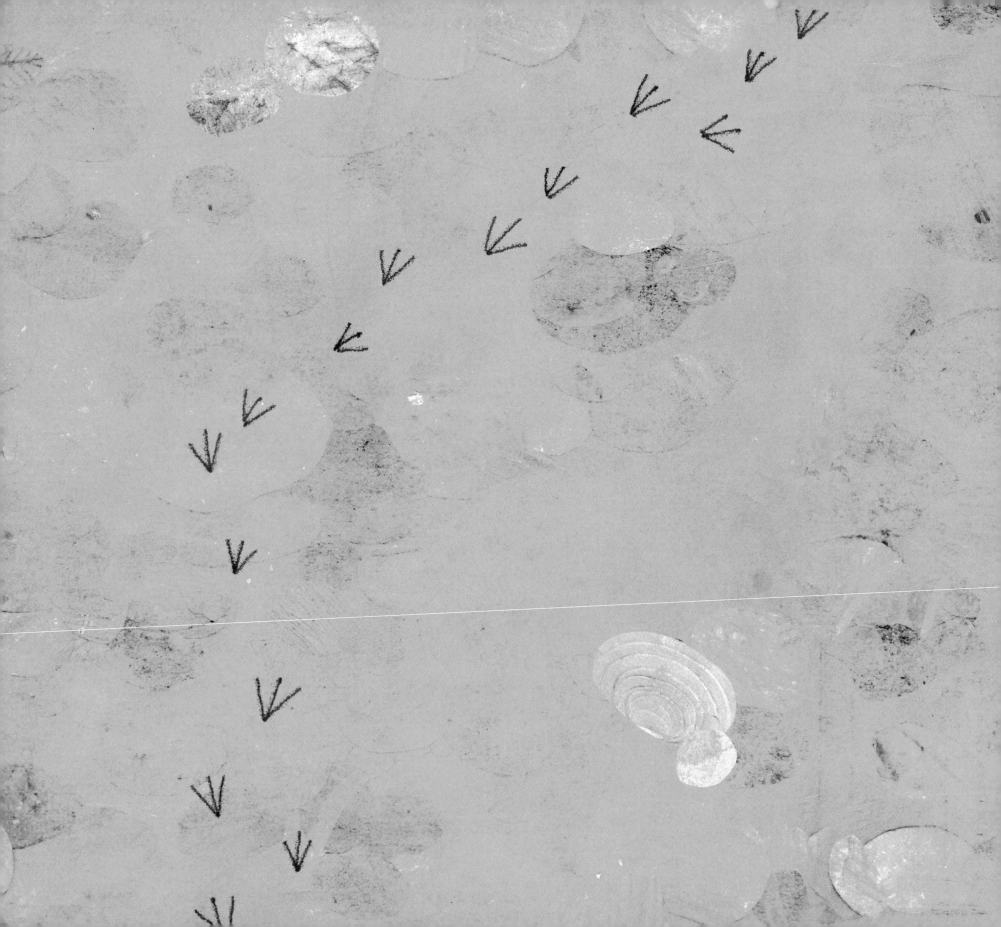